CW00833077

THE WITCH OF CRIMSON ARROWS

THE OKRITH NOVELLAS

AK MULFORD

Copyright © 2021 by AK Mulford

All rights reserved.

No part of this book may be reproduced in any form or by any electronic or
mechanical means, including information storage and retrieval systems,
without written permission from the author, except for the use of brief
quotations in a book review.

ISBN 978-0-473-58897-7

Publisher AK Mulford

2021

New Zealand

Cover designed by MiblArt

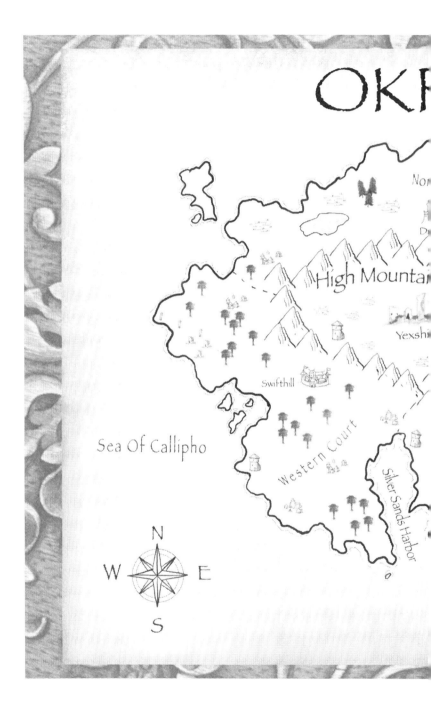

OKR

Nor

D

High Mountai

Yexshi

Swifthill

Sea Of Callipho

Western Court

Silver Sands Harbor

N
W   E
S

ITH

n Court

an

Sea of Wetamuir

ourt

Rotted Peak

Eastern Court

Wynreach

uthern Court

Crushwold

Saxbridge

CHAPTER ONE

The warm summer air wafted the peppery scent of tavern cooking out its back door. Remy took a breath, looking up to the swollen blue moon in the sky.

Hands fisted in her skirt, hauling Remy back against a warm chest.

Burly arms encircled her as an ale-laden breath whispered in her ear, "Meet me at the old mill tonight."

She wouldn't have let him grab her if she didn't know who he was. She could smell the shoe polish from a mile away.

Edgar.

Remy turned around to face the brawny blond. He was handsome for a human. At twenty-two, the locals still called Edgar "the cobbler's son"; he had yet to make a name for himself in the family business. He wasn't built like a cobbler. He was built like an ox.

The hot summer air swirled around them in the shadows outside the Windy Oak tavern.

"I don't know if I'll be able to get away tonight," Remy hedged as Edgar ran his hands over her sides.

"Find a way," Edgar demanded, pressing himself up against her. She could feel his hard length through their clothes. "I want you tonight."

This was what Remy loved about Edgar. He wasn't much of a romantic lover, but he was her first. Remy didn't understand all the songs and poems about the beauty of love. But his animalistic need for her—that kept her going to those secret rendezvous at the old mill.

Her guardian, Heather, taught Remy her entire life to keep her head down. She was never allowed to draw attention. Having this one little secret with Edgar was everything to her, a lifeline. Permitting herself his full attention, letting him touch her. Even if he could only get so close, it made her feel alive, like she was worthy of one small indulgence at least. There was some point to her existence other than hiding.

"Okay, okay." Remy curled up her plump lips, her warm brown hands drifting up to Edgar's shoulders. "I will meet you there in an hour."

"An hour," Edgar groaned, but he released his grip on Remy's skirt.

"Wait for me," Remy whispered up to him with a devious smirk.

"Always." Edgar smiled with half-hooded eyes.

She pushed away from him and scampered back inside the Windy Oak. Her heart skipped inside her chest. Sneaking around always did that to her. It was a tiny thrill in her otherwise mundane life. She was eighteen years old and had only kissed one boy before Edgar. That kiss had led to their immediate departure from the town. Heather and Fenrin, her brown witch companions, wouldn't like what she was doing with Edgar, but she didn't care. Why couldn't she have this one small thing?

The Windy Oak was still lively inside, but slowing. The remaining patrons were all drunk. A brawl broke out in the center of the room. A glass smashed against the wall beside Remy's head. She didn't even flinch. It was going to be that kind of night then.

The matron of the Windy Oak, Magda, sat at the bar, her face pressed into the bar-top, eyes rolling back in her head, lost to the bottle of spirits in her hand. She would be of no help.

"Alright, alright, break it up," the barman called, throwing a rag over his shoulder and grabbing a wooden club from behind the bar. He was a gruff, balding man, tall and even wider. Krober was his name. Remy had never learned if it was his surname or given name, but either way, she didn't like it.

Using his large belly, Krober pushed into the crowd. Grabbing one of the brawlers by the ear, he said, "Go home, Jacob," and tossed the man onto the floor.

He pointed his club in a circle to the rest of the men. Each withdrew a step.

"Now you can stay and drink, or you can go," he said in a thick Western Court accent. "But there'll be no more fighting. Got it?"

The men all nodded in agreement. One went pale and bent over, releasing the contents of his stomach onto the floor.

"Great," a voice sounded from beside Remy.

Fenrin stood leaning against the wall beside her. Her lanky friend with golden hair was so tall that his head rested above the doorframe. He crossed his arms as he watched Krober break up the fight.

Fenrin and Remy were the same age. Heather had taken in the young brown witch when he was twelve after finding him orphaned on the street. Neither Heather nor Fenrin meant it to be a permanent thing. And yet here he was six years later, still with the two of them.

The smell of stomach acid and rotten ale filled the room. Remy was so used to the reek of it that her stomach didn't even clench anymore. She promised herself once more that she would never touch a drink. She stared disappointedly as the men filtered out of the tavern, emptying it for the night.

"Time to clean up." She sighed, tying up her loose black curls. She grabbed a mop and bucket from the corner while Fenrin grabbed a broom and dustpan.

Krober made his way back to the empty bar, giving Fenrin's ass a smack as he went. Fenrin frowned but didn't jump. The barman smacked his bony ass so often that he was used to it. Fenrin couldn't wait until they moved on from the Windy Oak to the next tavern. They never stayed in a place for more than three years, just in case someone figured out what kind of witch Remy truly was.

The Windy Oak was disgusting, the staff equally so. But at least Magda did not expect them to do much in the way of cleaning, just the broken glass and the human fluids, both of which Remy had cleaned off these floors at one point or another.

Remy got to work, thinking of her rendezvous with Edgar instead of the mop in her hands. As she moved the mop across the floor, there was a snap above her head. She felt the punch to the crown of her head before she registered what it was. A lantern clanged across the floor, white candle wax strewn about her feet.

"Gods," Remy cursed, reaching up to the back of her

neck. Hot candle wax hardened in a trail down her shoulder. She looked up at the broken twine string above her head.

"Who hangs lanterns with twine anyway?" She scowled as the lump on her head began to throb. "I hate this bloody place."

"Remy, your hands," Fenrin whispered.

Remy shoved her fists into her pockets without even looking at them. She knew what she would see. A pulsing red glow would be encircling her hands. She could feel the magic buzzing through her fingertips.

"What was that noise?" Krober called, popping up from behind the bar.

Remy closed her eyes, spinning so her back was to him. She could feel the vibration behind her eyes. She knew they would be filled with that magical red glow too. All witches glowed the color of their magic: brown, blue, green, and red. The magic flared in response to heightened emotions, not only negative ones like fear and anger, but positive ones like joy and pleasure too.

Vostemur, the Northern Court king, put a bounty on any red witch head delivered to him, and many witch hunters still sought out that colossal payday even twelve years later. Remy's scarlet glow would be a dead giveaway.

She could hear Fenrin step closer, blocking her from Krober's line of sight. "Just a fallen lantern. A few wax burns. She's fine."

"Ah well," Krober grumbled, looking at the dented metal lantern on the floor. "You'd better be cleaning that up too then."

The barman moved to the back door and pushed his way to the kitchens. Remy took another deep breath, willing away that red buzzing. When she was certain it was gone, she turned back to Fenrin.

Those deep blue eyes stared back at her through heavily furrowed brows. "That was too close, Remy."

"I didn't expect a burning lantern to fall from the sky, did I?" she snarled, rubbing the burn mark on her neck again.

"I thought you had this under control." Fenrin's wary eyes held Remy's gaze. Fenrin had seen Remy's red magic a dozen times before, but she tried to hide it from even him. Sometimes she longed to practice using it, but she never did. The stakes of anyone seeing her were too high.

"I do have this under control," Remy said, dropping her voice into a growl. She tucked a stray curl back behind her ear.

"Try harder then," Fenrin groused even as he grabbed the mop out of Remy's hand and began cleaning up the filthy floor.

Remy wanted to shout at him, but she knew the anger would wake that urge for magic again.

She had already failed once that night to keep her powers under control. If she wanted to keep her head attached to her body, she could not fail at it again.

CHAPTER TWO

They hiked with ease up the mountainside. Fenrin used to struggle to match Remy's pace, but, thanks to his growth spurt, he now kept up effortlessly. They made haste towards the lookout ahead. It was the one good thing about this terrible town. They had a hiking trail up into the Western Court slopes of the High Mountains. A half-hour walk up led to a beautiful sweeping vista of thin waterfalls dropping from the mountains. They stopped a few times to drink handfuls of water from the fresh mountain streams. There was magic in these waters, Remy knew. Hiking up to the waterfalls with Fenrin, she could feel the spirit of Yexshire, the capital city of the High Mountain Court.

Okrith was in the center of the continent of the High Mountain Court. The people living outside the halo of mountains didn't have a name for each peak, calling them only the High Mountains. But her people had names for each of the twelve largest summits that circled the High Mountain Court like a crown. Remy knew they were now climbing the western side of Mount Ospian. On the other side of this sacred mountain was the burial site of her ancestors.

As they moved up the trail, Remy could feel her family's spirits. She yearned to tunnel straight through the mountainside. Then she would be home. To be this close filled her with nostalgia. The fresh air, the earthy forest smell, the familiar sounds of birdsong: it all reminded her of Yexshire. The higher they got toward the summit of Mount Ospian, the closer Remy was to her true home.

She didn't know if she would ever see it again. The steep jagged peaks of Mount Ospian were impenetrable, so high they were permanently covered in snow. She would never make it over the top. A western road into Yexshire once existed through the saddle of the mountains between Ospian and Asdievan. Hennen Vostemur, the fae king of the Northern Court, blocked them now. The mountain pass was filled in with loose sliding rock, the entire road covered in thick brambles. Even if someone was brave enough to trek through the western road to Yexshire, Remy's homeland was still rife with Northern looters even twelve years after the Siege of Yexshire.

They turned the final corner, and the wilderness opened to a view of the mountain. Small waterfalls sprung from the mountain itself, falling like salt from a shaker, far down into a small pond below. The forest crowded around it, dense and hungry for the life-giving water. The wind swirled the spray, casting rainbows among the mist. The sun beamed from the cloudless blue sky.

Every time Remy saw this place, something in her sighed, like a fist unclenching in the center of her chest. She had lit many candles in her life, but being here was the closest to a holy experience she had ever felt. Fenrin perched himself on a fallen log and Remy followed. They sat in that same spot every time, catching their breath and watching in awe.

It had become their special place, the two of them. They came here at least once a week. Being fully immersed in the forest was one of the few times Remy felt truly safe. She could look in every direction and would not see a single sign of human, witch, or fae life, not a smokestack or washing line. She couldn't smell the ale and bile and horse manure. She couldn't hear the loud bustling of busy, grumpy townsfolk, the clucking of chickens, or the screeching wheels of a rusty cart.

Here it was calm.

After a long silence, Fenrin reached over into the bushes behind him and started picking blackberries. He had found a bush downhill from the path the year before and decided to move some canes of it up to their secret spot. This summer they had eaten fresh wild berries while watching the waterfalls. He passed Remy a handful in his large hand, and she smirked at him. This was the benefit of having a brown witch as her best friend.

"I will have a huge garden in Yexshire," Remy said, shoving a berry into her mouth. Its sweet tang burst onto her tongue. They tasted far better up here than the ones foraged near the town. Even the soil didn't like that seedy village. But the fae didn't like seedy villages either, so the town was mostly human, apart from the occasional witch. The races of witches and humans intermingled occasionally but the fae set themselves apart. They were the wealthiest race, too, ruling each of the five courts of Okrith, living in castles and counting their gold.

"And a strawberry patch too," Fenrin added through his berry-stained lips. He finished his handful of berries and reached for more.

"Yes, definitely." Remy smiled. "We will eat berries and cream for dessert every night on the balcony as we watch the sun set over the mountains."

This was their usual routine. They would sit there, eating berries and talking about the lives they would live once the Northern King was defeated.

"What about horses?" Fenrin asked.

"What about horses?" Remy looked at Fenrin sideways.

"You should have a stable with horses," Fenrin said. "You've never mentioned that before."

They had a detailed dream of the castle they would build. They knew what every room would look like, down to the paintings they would hang on the walls. Every time they climbed up here, they would add more to their dream home.

"I don't know how to ride horses." Remy frowned. They never had enough money to keep a horse, though fleeing from tavern to tavern would be easier if they didn't always have to do it on foot.

"You could learn." Fenrin insisted. "We'd hire an amazing tutor and buy only the most patient horses."

Remy couldn't help but laugh. These were the logistics that she was hung up on? The horse riding? She was fine to dream of a world where King Vostemur was dead and the High Mountain Court thrived again, where she and Fenrin had all the money in the world . . . but she couldn't imagine herself riding a horse?

"Fine," Remy relented. "There shall be stables for the horses that pull our enormous carriages."

"How many carriages will we own?" Fenrin grinned.

"Four, naturally." Remy laughed. "One for long travels, one for short trips, one for everyday use, and a grand one just to show off."

Fenrin chuckled, wiping his hands on his stone-gray trousers. The hemline now sat mid-shin on his legs.

"And we'd buy you some clothing that actually fits you," Remy said, eyeing his bare legs, covered in dark blonde hair.

"Oh, come now," Fenrin tutted. "We will have our very own seamstress who will design all of our decadent attire. Although I shall have the final say, otherwise you would only wear teal."

"What is wrong with teal?" Remy pouted.

"Nothing, but your people will find you too eccentric if you only ever wear one color." Fenrin snorted.

Her people. This was part of their fantasy too. They were the King and Queen of Yexshire. The thought of Fenrin in a crown never failed to make Remy laugh. This daydream had started the year they first met when they were twelve and he had learned who Remy really was. Only two people in the whole world knew of her red witch powers, Fenrin and Heather. Twelve-year-old Fenrin had immediately declared that he would be the next king of Yexshire, and so their daydreaming began.

"And what will your people think of the clothes you choose?" Remy jeered. "I don't think their king will have much of a sense of style either."

"Only because I've never had the money for it." Fenrin wiggled his eyebrows at her. "But we will hire the finest stylist, of course."

His far-reaching arms picked a few leaves off a bush to his right.

"Here." He passed one to her while popping two more in his mouth.

Remy looked down to the waxy leaf and frowned but put it in her mouth anyway. It had a spicy taste.

"What's this for?" she asked. Heather and Fenrin were

always giving her leaves and berries and flowers to eat. They could identify every single thing that grew out of the Western Court forests, the native homeland of the brown witches.

"It's a warming remedy. It will help fend off colds as the autumn chill comes." He grabbed a few more and stuffed them in his pocket to bring back to their lodgings. He would dry them, powder them, and mix them in a tincture of oils. Then he would sell them to the locals.

"It's still summer," Remy groused. "I'm not ready to talk about autumn."

She waited all year for summer, her favorite season. She didn't care for the heat or humidity, but she would bear it for the sunshine. In Yexshire the sun shined every day, even when there were huge banks of snow on the ground. The storms would come, but always the sun would peek out from behind the clouds, even if only for an hour. Her skin craved the sun's kiss. In the high altitude of the mountains, the sun's rays were stronger, and she craved it more than anything, more than food, or a soft bed, or safety.

The Western Court could go months without a hint of sun. It was nearly paralyzing, living in the gloom of those dark gray winters. It made Remy feel like a bird trying to hide as a fish. She was not meant for this place.

The bitter aftertaste of the leaf in her mouth made Remy grimace. "How can you possibly remember all these things? Or do brown witches just instinctively know?"

"I've been learning the medicinal properties of the forests since before I could walk." Fenrin's face washed over with a far-away look. His eyes drifted beyond the waterfall, beyond sight itself, and deep back into some memory.

Fenrin didn't talk about his past much. Remy knew it was a sore point for him as much as it was for her. And yet she wished they could talk about it. He was the only person in her life she was allowed to talk to.

"Do you remember your mother?" she asked quietly. She didn't know why she said it. Maybe she wanted him to ask her about her own mother. Remy thought she remembered her mother's face, but it felt like trying to grab a handful of fog. She never fully got the image. Remy had been six when her mother died. People had always told her before the Siege of Yexshire that she looked just like her mother. Every time she looked in the mirror, she wondered if she still did. Was it her mother's brown eyes flecked with green staring back at her?

"Of course I remember my mother," Fenrin growled. His whole countenance darkened. Remy knew she shouldn't have asked. "It was only six years ago."

"What happened to her?" Remy pushed, biting her lip.

"Why are you ruining this?" Fenrin hissed as he gestured out to their special place. He wouldn't talk to Remy about it, not even after six years, not even here in this place where it was only the two of them. Some wounds never healed.

"I'm sorry," Remy said, looking at her hands. "I thought maybe you'd want to talk about it one day."

"Well, you were wrong." Fenrin's voice was something like she had never heard before, like a wounded animal readying to lash out and bite her.

Fenrin shot to his feet.

"It's getting late. We should head back before our shift starts," he said, moving past Remy back toward the trail. They had at least another hour before they had to leave.

"Fenrin, please," Remy said, moving around him to block his way. She stared all the way up at him, into those blue eyes. "I'm sorry. I won't ask again. I just. . . ." Remy wouldn't cry. She refused to let herself feel it. But the thought of Fenrin not speaking to her was too much to take. "You are my only friend. Please don't be mad at me."

Fenrin's shoulders dropped at that, releasing the anger he was holding so tightly.

"I'm sorry too," he said, staring down at her and then dropping his gaze to his too small boots. "Her name was Rose. She died, Remy. That's all I want to say about it."

She swallowed and bobbed her chin. She suspected the means of his mother's death. She had for a long time. His rawness made Remy wonder if his mother had taken her own life, but Fenrin had never confirmed it.

Remy reached out and squeezed Fenrin's hand, making him look to her again.

"We will need a personal cobbler too, because your feet will never stop growing." She grinned. Fenrin's face finally melted into a soft smile.

Then she remembered. *Cobbler*. *Edgar*.

Shit.

She had forgotten to sneak out and meet him at the old mill last night. He would be furious with her this morning. It was not the first time she had forgotten him, but he should have known what he was getting himself into. She had been too exhausted after cleaning up and bathing away the stink of the day. She had slipped into bed, completely forgetting about the cobbler's son. Remy did not feel an ounce of guilt. This was who she was, take it or leave it, and she knew he would take it.

CHAPTER THREE

T he Windy Oak was quiet midweek. The locals
had filtered out by midnight. Lavinia sat perched
at the bar, trying to drag stories out of the two
travelers who had arrived late in the evening. Fenrin leaned
over the bar to listen to them talk.

"I swear to you, they grow plums the size of my fist in
the Southern Capital," the portly man said through a
mouthful of roast chicken.

Lavinia laughed with delight. Midnight was like
morning for that nocturnal creature. But with one married,
older couple in the tavern, her pockets would not be heavy
with coins tonight.

"It's true," the woman with umber brown skin added.
Her Southern accent was so thick it took Remy a second to
realize she was still speaking Ific, the common tongue
spoken by both humans and fae. "The Southern palace sits
right at the tip of the Southern Court. It has the most fertile
soil you've ever seen. Good growing there. Plenty of rain,
never a frost."

"Does it truly never snow there?" Lavinia said in a

muffled voice. Her mouth held four hair pins as she rummaged around her coiffed head to find the last ones so she could finally let down her auburn locks.

The rest of the tavern was dark and silent. Remy ambled around the room, slowly blowing out candles so she could listen to their stories. She had never been to the Southern Court and loved hearing tales about it.

"I've heard you don't even need a cloak at night," Lavinia added, unburdening herself of her heavy necklace.

"Nah, in the very south of the kingdom, maybe," the man said through another mouthful of food. He nodded over to the courtesan. "You could make a fine living in the Southern Court."

"That's the dream." Lavinia sighed longingly. "Maybe one day."

"Life doesn't happen from *maybe one days*, Chicken," the woman said. She leaned over the bar to Fenrin. He leaned in toward her with an arched brow.

"The West is giving my knees a real hard time," the woman said in a low voice. She slid a copper coin across the table to him. "You know of any brown witches in these parts who can sort me out?"

This was a usual occurrence in taverns—the buying and selling of witch services. You could ask the barman at any tavern, and they'd procure you a healing balm or sleep elixir. The Western Court was the native home to the brown witches, though they spread all over the continent of Okrith. The Southern Court had green witches who specialized in vitality and virility. They made gardens grow, delicious food, and many a potion to aide in the bedroom. The green witches flourished perfectly in the Southern Court, where everything was a celebration.

Fenrin smiled as he picked up the coin off the bar.

"I'll be right back," he said with a bob of his head.

He disappeared out the back door to the kitchens. Remy frowned. She was jealous she wasn't allowed to participate in their witch business. Heather tried to assure Remy she was still a help to them, but Remy knew she was a burden. They would be thriving in one of the beautiful West Coast towns were it not for her. Remy heard many a traveler talk about the beauty of the ocean, and she craved seeing it for herself. At most, she had only ever seen it as a sliver on the horizon.

"So, what does a girl such as yourself do on a quiet night like this?" the woman asked Lavinia. The courtesan was now wiping down her heavy layer of rouge, using a bar glass as a mirror.

"You wouldn't have quiet nights if you went south, I'm telling you," the man interjected, and his wife elbowed him.

"Probably head home and do some mending and washing. Very exciting." Lavinia chuckled. "And dream of finding my prince and riding off into the sunset."

She mimed a crown on her head, lifting her nose in the air with a giggle.

"I've seen Prince Raffiel, you know," the man said, puffing out his chest.

The courtesan gasped.

"Oh, don't get him started," the man's wife groused.

This was a tale told around every inn and bar in Okrith: the sightings of Raffiel Dammacus, the Crown Prince of the High Mountain Court. They were little more than fairy tales, but Remy loved hearing them nevertheless. She strolled closer toward the bar, pretending to rearrange the saltshakers on the tables.

Fae had always been the ruling class. The High Mountain Court had been the most powerful in all the five fae courts. What made the High Mountain fae special was that they had both fae and red witch magic. They were the only fae in all of Okrith to wield witch magic, and the jealousy of the other courts was incessant.

Hennen Vostemur, King of the Northern Court, was now the most powerful king in the realm. He had resented the High Mountain Court's powers and the elite coven of red witches who followed them. The red witches had melded their powers with the fae's own, making them both incredibly powerful.

All fae had once revered the High Mountain Court. Likewise, all witch covens had once esteemed the red witches. That fae-witch alliance had ruled peacefully over the High Mountain Court. But after the Siege of Yexshire, all the High Mountain fae and red witches were slaughtered . . . well, nearly all of them.

The sound of laughter at the bar pulled Remy back from her swirling thoughts.

"He has not seen the Dammacus prince." The woman rolled her eyes.

"I have," her husband said.

Rumors were whispered that only one High Mountain fae had survived the Siege of Yexshire: the eldest son of King and Queen Dammacus. People claimed they saw him fleeing the burning castle, but no one knew for certain. Gossip spread from town to town over the years, claiming he had been spotted. But whenever King Vostemur sent soldiers to investigate, nothing turned up.

"He is a ghost," the woman said, swatting her husband's shoulder.

"Then why can't Vostemur use the Immortal Blade then, eh?"

Despite the Northern King's ongoing efforts, he could not wield the Immortal Blade. The sword of power was linked by blood magic to the High Mountain fae. Only once every one of their bloodline had died could another fae wield it. With that blade, Vostemur could rule the continent. So, the hunt for Prince Raffiel continued even twelve years later.

"It is all nonsense," the woman insisted as Fenrin came back to the bar. He slid the brown glass vial over the counter to her with a smile. "Those witch hunters even said as much."

The curling of Fenrin's fingers was the only indication he gave of surprise. "You've seen witch hunters?"

"Oh, don't worry, Dear." The woman patted Fenrin's hand. "They were two towns over in Barmouth, and they seemed sharp enough. They wouldn't mistake *you* for a red witch."

Remy went wholly still. Each heartbeat was a hammer to her chest. She could tell Fenrin's attention was on her, even though he didn't dare look up at her.

Fenrin reached his hand to his stomach.

"You know, I'm feeling a bit queasy. Probably those dodgy clams at the market." He looked over to Remy. "I think we better go home, Rem."

"I am not the one stupid enough to eat clams in the market." Remy crossed her arms. Witch hunters were a problem, but they were two towns away. The likelihood of them stumbling into the Windy Oak was low.

"Aw, go see the lad home," Lavinia called to her. "There's no work to be had here."

Remy put down the saltshakers and followed Fenrin out the back door. She didn't want to hear any more stories of the ghost prince or the witch hunters anyway. She didn't want to hear the grand tales and be reminded of her unimportance.

※

"We should be working," Remy said in Mhenbic, the witches' native tongue. "We don't have the money to be taking days off for a threat that isn't even in this town."

"We could all use a break. Especially you." Fenrin snorted from a stool in the corner.

"What's that supposed to mean?" Remy snarled, wanting to turn her head but having to hold still as Heather braided her hair. Remy's guardian was a beautiful witch, with copper-red hair and warm hazel eyes. She had smooth pale skin, her deep smile lines the only indication that she was middle-aged.

The two of them sat tucked up near the threadbare curtains on the living room floor.

They had secured lodging across town from the Windy Oak in an unsavory apartment building. Remy was sure most of the tenants were criminals, but they were the kind of drunken criminals that didn't cause too much trouble and didn't ask questions.

It was bigger than some of their previous lodgings. It even had its own bathing chamber, but it was damp and reeked of mold. The windows all had holes around the sills, and it was impossible to keep the place warm. The three of them all slept in the one large bed in the winter, but in the summer Fenrin preferred to sleep in the cluttered room next to the bedroom which served as kitchen, dining, and living space.

"I saw the baker wink at you when he was delivering the morning loaves," Fenrin ratted.

Remy balled up her fists. He was always getting involved in Remy's business.

"He did *not* wink at me," she hissed.

The only light came from the candles flickering on the dining table, casting long shadows throughout the room.

Remy stretched out her legs in front of her with a frustrated sigh. She leaned against the stained armchair. The furniture had been infested with all manner of creatures when they first moved in, but Heather had dealt with that quickly. The brown witch had whipped up a potion—a strong-scented mixture of marigold, cloves, and thyme, which drove the pests away. It was another benefit of having brown witches as companions.

"He absolutely did wink," Fenrin insisted, not letting it go.

He strode over to the kitchen countertop and grabbed a dried bundle of lavender. He set it down on the dining table, careful to avoid the candles' flames. The table's surface was covered in half-made potions. Fenrin stripped the lavender flowers from their stems and put them into his mortar. He grabbed the pestle without even looking and began grinding the flowers into a powder.

They made enough money to get by. They could have moved to bigger taverns closer to the Western Court cities if they had wanted to, but their goal was to stick to the backcountry where the living was rough and the money was bad . . . and it was all because Remy was a red witch.

"You must be careful around that baker," Heather said, pulling pieces of Remy's hair into her braid. Heather's hands moved easily with the practice of many years. The brown witch always wore her copper hair in a braided bun at the nape of her neck and insisted that Remy slept with her hair in a braid to keep it from tangling. Heather had spent too many years trying to brush the knots out of Remy's curly hair as a child to let her wear it down.

"I've seen the way he looks at you too." Heather scolded, as if the baker's looks were Remy's fault.

"He doesn't look at me like anything," Remy protested. She jerked her head forward in exasperation, yanking her hair in Heather's hands. Remy pulled out her totem bag from the pocket in the lining of her dress and began passing it back and forth between her hands.

Witches used to wear their totem bags around their necks, but now they kept them hidden in secret pockets in the lining of their clothes. The necklaces had been a visible symbol that signaled the wearer was a witch. It was a dangerous thing to be a witch in Okrith now. It was harder to spot the difference between a witch and a human without the necklaces, and no one wanted to draw the attention of the fae anymore. Still, many of the witches kept the little black pouches on them for luck. Most of the objects were personal only to them. They would rotate some of the totems out on the full moons, but some always stayed.

Remy felt the usual clink in her hands as she shifted the sack back and forth. She could feel the outline of the snail shell. It was given to her by Morganna, a fallen red witch. Morganna told her the snail shell would bring her patience, a fitting gift for a boisterous five-year-old. Her totem bag also had a fledgling feather from a High Mountain hawk and a long piece of red string used to make witch ribbons. The ribbons flew atop the Temple of Yexshire as a symbol of hope for the future. The red string didn't make Remy feel very hopeful anymore. She didn't use the crimson string for prayers, she used it for tying the fletching to her arrows.

"We need more corn oil," Fenrin grumbled, wiping bits of lavender powder off his crumpled brown tunic.

"I have done nothing to encourage the baker," Remy said, even though the conversation had moved on. She did that a lot, getting so lost in her thoughts that she didn't respond until much later.

"Good," Fenrin said as he grabbed a sprig of rosemary.

In the past few years, Fenrin had appointed himself another unwanted protector alongside Heather. Remy didn't tell Fenrin about male attention anymore. She had made that mistake the first time she had kissed a farm boy. She was fifteen, and Fenrin had ratted her out immediately to Heather. They left that village in the night and Remy had received such a long-winded lecture from Heather that she never mentioned her crushes on boys and girls to Fenrin again. If they ever found out about Edgar, she'd never hear the end of it.

"Good," Heather added, finishing Remy's hair.

The brown witch moved to the corner where their hiking packs rested and began repacking her clothes from the day.

Heather insisted that they kept their bags packed, resetting them every night, so they were always ready to leave at a moment's notice, in case Remy's identity was discovered. It was easy enough since they had very few possessions. When an article of clothing was beyond mending, they bartered for a new one. Remy was allowed one book, so she always picked the biggest, longest tales possible to make it last. Heather would roll her eyes when Remy would lament leaving a book behind.

"I know you know what is at stake if it is discovered you are not a brown witch," Heather added more to herself as she packed.

Fenrin hummed to himself at the table.

"And yet you insist on reminding me." Remy turned to

glare at Heather. "I like my head attached to my body, thank you very much. I will gladly keep away from the baker. And you two can stop acting like mother hens. I don't need you to remind me."

Remy clenched her totem bag so tight she thought the snail shell might crack. She shot up and stormed off to the bedroom. It wasn't very satisfying storming off to a shared bedroom. Remy debated leaving but it wouldn't be worth another passive aggressive conversation with Heather.

CHAPTER FOUR

"Alright gentlemen, what'll it be?" Krober said to the two burly men who sat at the bar. Lavinia had pushed in instantly, ready to beguile them.

Heather stood amongst the tables, selling little vials from her deep pockets to the patrons. Quite a few hangover cures were already being sold, and it was still midday. There must be a celebration happening. Remy braced herself for a long night. The money was adequate when the tavern was busy, it kept them going during the leaner times when the travelers slowed through the village and the locals kept indoors against the winter chill.

Remy wasn't ready for the winter. She never was. She didn't mind the cold or the snow, but soon she'd be looking up to the sky and wondering if the sun slipping behind the clouds would be the last time she'd see it for another four months.

She shook the thought from her head. It was still summer. She couldn't live that far in the future, especially in a place like this. She didn't know what her life would be from one year to the next. She didn't even know what she could hope for it to be. Eventually, Heather and Fenrin would get sick of hiding with her. They'd move to bigger towns and have a better life, and Remy would carry on alone, hiding in the Western Court. She debated it a lot, leaving them behind, running away so that they would be free of her. She wondered every day if Heather regretted taking her in.

"Remy!" Magda called from the kitchens. She held her thumb up, pointing to the back door.

Remy cringed. She knew who would be waiting out there. Even from across the room she felt Heather's hazel eyes on her, as if her guardian also knew who was waiting out back. At least Fenrin was cleaning upstairs, or she'd have two eagles' eyes upon her.

Remy plodded through the kitchens, brushing her hands down her apron as she went.

"Don't take too long," Magda grumbled as Remy headed to the back doorway.

Standing outside, grumpy as anything, was Edgar. He leaned against the outer wall of the Windy Oak, arms crossed, frowning down at the ground.

"You can't be asking for me here, Edgar," Remy reprimanded instead of apologizing. They had agreed that they would meet in secret. He'd visit her in the shadows and nothing more. Asking at the tavern's back door was going to be a problem.

Edgar looked up at Remy with steely blue eyes.

"Where have you been the last two days?" he ground out, like she had betrayed him in some deep way.

"I forgot the other night. I fell asleep," Remy said. Edgar let out a growl of frustration. "Hey," Remy said straightening. This man was not entitled to any of her. She was not even his girlfriend, and yet he acted like she had done something terrible. "I was in here until 3 am cleaning vomit off the floors. You would be tired too. Last night Fenrin was sick, and I had to take care of him."

The lie rolled easily off Remy's tongue.

Edgar released his fists, clenched at his sides. She was not about to let some selfish little boy make her feel bad.

"Tonight then," Edgar said at last, and Remy rolled her eyes. It was all he could think about. Still, it thrilled her a bit, his desperation to get between her legs. There was a power there.

"I don't know," Remy said coyly with a smirk even though she knew already that she would agree.

"Come on, Remy," Edgar said, backing her up to the tavern wall. His arms caged her in as he stared down with those burning, lustful eyes. This was why she put up with Edgar. When he looked down at her like that, his muscled arms framing her body, his eyes filled with an unsated desire that made her feel alive. He looked at her as if he were a dying man and she was the cure. That was why she indulged him.

"Fine," Remy said, lifting her long dark lashes to peek up at him. "I shouldn't be too late tonight."

Edgar's hands slid up the sides of her dress and stilled over her breasts, making her nipples stiffen. Edgar was not subtle. He was a greedy man, but something in Remy loved surrendering to that. Her life was so controlled. Every movement, every word she uttered, was planned in advance to keep her safe. Releasing all those layers made her feel free. Giving herself over to someone who wanted her so badly felt like she was taking a measure of control for herself.

Edgar's warm lips brushed over Remy's full ones as he

dropped his hands. He gave her a soft, fleeting kiss and said, "See you tonight, love."

He trudged back down the dirt road. Remy watched as he disappeared down the long lane of single-story houses, each one more derelict than the next. Her cheeks flushed, her head spinning. It felt good to feel so dizzy. She took a couple steadying breaths and moved back inside.

Fenrin waited, leaning against the kitchen table. Remy froze, dropping her eyes to her feet for a brief moment. She hoped Fenrin didn't note the move, but she knew he would. The kitchen bustled around them in preparation for the dinner rush, but Fenrin and Remy stood there stock still in the eye of the storm.

Fenrin stared at the wall ahead, brushing his bottom lip with his thumb.

"What are you up to, Fen?" Remy tried to sound casual. The back door to the kitchens had been shut. Surely, he hadn't heard what she had been saying? He didn't have the fae's incredible hearing. How could he possibly know anything about what she was doing? She answered her own question instantly in her mind. She wasn't being careful enough. She was letting Edgar get too close.

"Just finished upstairs," Fenrin said turning his dark blue eyes to Remy. His eyes were a different shade of blue than Edgar's. Fenrin's eyes were the color of twilight, warm and rich. Edgar's eyes were paler. They didn't contain Fenrin's depth.

"Okay, good." Remy chewed her bottom lip. The long stretch of uncomfortable silence between them made her hackles raise, ready to defend herself.

"I've come down to help bring out the food at Hilda's request." Fenrin nodded to the cook scrambling behind him. Hilda moved like a spider, her hands shifting pans and bowls with such speed it seemed she had more than two limbs. Remy had wondered if Hilda had been a glamoured fae many times, seeing how quickly she moved. But when Remy reached out with her magic, there was no buzzing in response. Hilda was a human. The Windy Oak had struck gold in finding her. She was worth at least four regular workers.

Hilda tossed plated trays of food on the bench behind Fenrin, ready for him to carry out into the dining hall. Remy stepped up next to Fenrin to grab one of the trays. Fenrin placed his hand gently over Remy's, stopping her from taking the tray. She looked up into those cautious eyes then.

"Whatever you're doing, Remy . . . ," he said softly and Remy yanked her hand away. This is what he had wanted to say? He was warning her.

"I have it under control, Fen," Remy growled.

"Do you?"

"You are not the boss of me, you don't get to tell me how to live my life," Remy hissed, balling her hands into fists.

"I do when it affects my life too." His face darkened as he matched Remy's posture.

"It only affects your life because you rat me out to Heather." Remy threw the words at him like a punch and watched them land. She would never let him forget what he had done.

They had been fifteen and living in a nice pastoral town. It was mostly farmland, but it had a tavern, the best place they had lived in many years. They found good lodgings with a garden out front, and they planted an herb garden for Heather and flowers for cutting that Remy decorated the house with. It was modest but beautiful, and Remy had loved it there.

Fenrin had taken it all away when he told Heather about Remy's first kiss. It was just a passing crush on a farm boy who ran a stand near the tavern. Remy barely ever saw him; she'd just linger a little longer to chat with him on her walks home.

One day when they were chatting, the boy leaned over and gave Remy a kiss on the lips. It was nothing more than a peck really, but it was her first kiss, and it made her whole body sing. Her magic hadn't glowed either. She'd managed to keep a tight lid on it, but she was so excited that a boy had kissed her, she had to tell someone. She ran home and told Fenrin, who wasn't happy for her at all. He was furious. He immediately told Heather, and Remy's guardian decided they had to leave at once. That's how they ended up in this rotten town for the last nearly three years, where the streets smelled like piss and people were more likely to spit on you than talk to you.

"Don't call me a rat!" Fenrin seethed, pulling Remy out of her sad nostalgia and back into her anger.

"You are a rat!" Remy shouted. "You're a fucking rat, Fenrin, and you ruin everything."

"Enough," Hilda shouted, her booming voice easily cutting above the sound of their bickering. "Bean pole," she said to Fenrin, "stop bickering with that sister of yours and take out my Gods damned food."

Sister. That was what they said she was, even though she looked nothing like Fenrin. Remy was tall and curvy. Fenrin was a giant skeleton. Remy had warm brown skin and Fenrin was as pale as milk. He had straight blond hair and Remy had loose black curls. There was no way they were siblings by blood, but Gods did they fight like they were.

Remy knew that neither of them would apologize. They never did after their squabbles. But they would cool off eventually, and after some unknown length of time they would start talking to each other again like nothing had happened. Remy hated Fenrin, and she loved him, and that was the closest thing she knew to a sibling.

Remy had two older brothers and one younger sister. All dead. Killed in the Siege of Yexshire. She wondered if she would fight with her real brothers like this. She vaguely remembered some arguments they had when she was a small child. Her brothers would get mad at her for following them around like a puppy dog. She wanted to do all the things that they were doing, and she was constantly a thorn in their sides. But she remembered them indulging her too, letting her look at their books or hold their toy weapons. She had felt so safe then. She had felt so certain that they would go on that way forever.

Remy bit down harder on the inside of her cheek and grabbed the tray of food in front of her. Enough of these memories. She had to go to work.

CHAPTER FIVE

Heather was already asleep when Remy entered the bedroom. Her guardian usually finished several hours before Remy and Fenrin. The brown witch had a bustling side business of witch remedies that meant she could only keep part-time hours at the tavern.

Remy peeled off her filthy work dress and put on her spare one. She needed to make sure she didn't get it dirty during her secret tryst with Edgar because she would need to wear it the next day while her current one dried. She was sick of dresses. They were too heavy and hard to move in. She promised herself the next time she needed clothes she would swap her dresses for tunics and trousers. It would be easy enough to convince Heather of it because tunics would draw even less attention to Remy.

She untied her thick curls, letting them cascade down her back. The smell of the tavern clung to her hair as she shook it out. She made her way back to the front room. Every surface was covered in brown witch wares. Baskets of dried herbs covered the table. More flowers and greens hung in the windows to dry, though the damp apartment made it take twice as long. The kitchen countertops held no food, but rather an assortment of brown glass vials, bottles of oils, and Fenrin's mortar and pestle. They didn't keep food for a number of reasons, including the mice that even Heather's magic could not keep at bay. Remy had begged Heather to get a cat but Heather had always denied her. Cats and witches went hand in hand and they didn't need to draw that kind of attention. Besides, Heather expected the tavern to feed them, so Remy and Fenrin worked every day in order to fill their bellies and when they did not, they foraged for their food along with their brown witch medicines.

"Where are you going?" Fenrin asked, ducking under the bathing chamber door.

Ugh. Remy had forgotten he was in there. She was too preoccupied. She had gotten pretty good at sneaking out that window, but not tonight.

"I'm going for a walk," Remy whispered so as not to wake Heather in the far room.

"It's three in the morning," Fenrin said.

"So?" Remy snarled back. Three in the morning was a normal time to be awake for both tavern workers and witches. Both were nocturnal.

Fenrin set his jaw to the side as he looked at her. In the last six months he had grown a whole foot taller, and his body had not kept up. His limbs were long and gangly, his frame incredibly lean despite the mountains of greasy tavern food he ate. He was the same age as Remy and twice her size. His height came in handy during tavern brawls, too. It was strange how patrons didn't want to mess with someone so tall, even though he could be snapped like a twig. Fenrin looked unusual enough that they didn't bother him.

"Should I come with you then?" Fenrin offered. Remy combed her fingers through her hair, hoping that her friend didn't suspect what she was up to.

"No, I should go alone . . . I'm going hunting," Remy said, moving toward her old, worn bow in the corner. She cursed herself quietly for thinking of that excuse. Now she'd have to bring home a rabbit or something before she could go to bed.

Remy forbade Fenrin from coming hunting with her. He could not keep still for the life of him, and he always scared her prey away.

Fenrin frowned at the bow and quiver of arrows. Remy had traded a huge chunk of her wages to acquire them, and still the weapon was aged and barely workable. She dreamed of buying a new maple bow and arrows made by a professional fletcher. But Remy was a skilled shot, and she found a way to make it work.

"We've got to put some meat on those bones after all," Remy added with a grin. Fenrin's grumpy disposition finally broke as he rolled his eyes at her little jab.

"Fine. Be home before sunrise or I'll come looking for you," he said. It was Remy's turn to roll her eyes.

"Ok, fine," Remy said, lifting the wobbly glass pane of the window. "Are we going to the waterfalls again in the morning?" she added.

Fenrin's face split into a full smile at that.

"I'll see you in an hour." Remy gave Fenrin a wink and ducked out the window. She could meet Edgar and catch a rabbit in an hour, no problem.

The moon hid behind thick clouds. The forest was dark and silent. Remy preferred it that way, alone in the darkness of the woods. She could still see enough to navigate through it when most human eyes could not. That made her safe. No fae came to this little town. It wasn't a main thoroughfare, and they didn't trade in any fine goods. Witches hardly passed through either.

Even the rabbits seemed to think they were safe in the stillness of the night. They had all come out of hiding. It was almost too easy to catch them, but Remy stopped at three, not wanting to waste her handmade arrows.

She tied the rabbits' feet together with a cord and carried on through the woods. She could see the old mill looming through the thick branches. It had been abandoned long ago, and the forest had surged up to reclaim it. Weeds and shrubs grew across its floors. Vines twined through open windows. It was the sort of place that humans feared and witches loved. But Edgar would venture out here even if he was afraid, his manhood overriding his sense of danger.

When Remy entered the large bottom floor of the mill, she tossed the rabbits and her bow and quiver on the dusty table. A nesting bat flew out into the night from above her. Remy huffed a laugh. Of course there would be a bat. The occult animals didn't seem to understand that witches liked to keep a low profile nowadays.

She reached under her skirt and slipped off her underpants, tucking them into her pocket. Sliding herself up onto a workbench top behind her, she waited.

Edgar was early too. She saw his flickering candle approaching through the woods. It made Remy chuckle. This human man trudging sightlessly through the forest to get to her, it made her feel powerful.

"Remy?" Edgar whispered into the darkness of the mill.

"Here," Remy called back making Edgar whirl around.

He stumbled blindly forward into the wooden table. Reaching out to steady himself, he placed his hand down right on top of a dead rabbit.

"Gah!" he barked, startling backwards.

"I told Fenrin I'd bring home dinner," Remy snickered.

Edgar held the candle higher and finally found her there.

"There you are, you little temptress." He grinned, making his way over to her and placing the candle beside her.

He bunched the fabric of her skirt into his fists and pulled her to him so her legs wrapped around his waist. Remy encircled her hands around his neck and pulled him into a kiss. He tasted like ale and mint leaves. He probably picked them along the way to hide his foul breath. Remy didn't really care much for kissing. It was too smelly and wet. Edgar's tongue pushed into her mouth, and she allowed it for a moment before turning her head into his shoulder and kissing his neck. It was an acceptable form of escape.

Edgar slid his hands under Remy's skirt and up her bare thighs. He groaned as his thumb brushed through the hair between her legs, finding her already bare for him. Remy loved that, how much she turned him on. His thumb found her center, sliding up and down as her breathing hitched. She wished he would keep going, attending to that perfect spot between her legs, but his hands retreated to his belt.

Edgar unbuckled his pants and released his hard length. Remy scooted herself to the edge of the work bench as Edgar positioned himself at her entrance. He pushed into her in one quick thrust. Remy gritted her teeth. It was a strange feeling having him fill her, one she never seemed to get used to. It was what everyone did. All the young people in this town were sneaking off to do this very thing. Some were so desperate for it too. It was all they talked about. Remy didn't understand it.

Edgar groaned again as he started to move himself in and out of her. Remy clung to the back of his shirt. The friction started to feel more pleasant. A warm wetness in her started building as Edgar's thrusts became more slick. Remy bit her lip. Okay, maybe she could understand it a little after all.

She rolled her head back. A faint buzzing began building in her eyes, and she was snapped out of her pleasure by the fear that they might begin to glow. She closed her eyes, just in case. She swept her hands under Edgar's shirt too, so that the glow wouldn't be seen in the darkness.

Edgar dropped his mouth to Remy's neck, kissing and sucking his way along her collarbone. Remy let out a soft hum. Each pump into her grew faster, deeper. A soft moan escaped her lips, making Edgar drive into her harder.

"How close are you?" he mumbled into her hair.

She knew what that meant. It meant that he was very close, and their little rendezvous was about to end.

"So close," Remy lied in a fake, breathy voice that she heard the courtesans using. Better to let him finish and get it over with. Then she would have time to finish by herself once he left. She was certain she had the better part of a half an hour left still.

Edgar moved faster again, gripping tight to Remy's dress. Remy moaned as he picked up a punishing speed. She knew she would be sore tomorrow. He was so close now. Remy began making all the gasps and groans she knew would set him over the top. The same sounds she would use to lie and say she reached her completion too.

But Edgar did something different this time. He released one hand from her dress and slid it back up under her skirt. His thumb pushed down on that spot right above where they joined and began moving in quick circles.

Remy moaned in earnest then, bucking against that hot, hard movement. She pinched her eyes further shut, certain she was glowing now. Her breathing came out in heavy pants as Edgar continued circling that bundle of nerves while thrusting deeply into her.

All at once Remy let out a cry, her climax bursting through her as Edgar quickly followed her over the edge. She was still tumbling into ecstasy when she felt Edgar's hard grip on her arm.

It happened so fast. One second they were deep in bliss, and the next Edgar pinned her hand to the wall next to her head. Remy's eyes flew open at that as Edgar stared at her hand and then her eyes in horror.

She was still glowing red.

Remy's heart leapt up into her mouth. The scarlet glow disappeared then, but Edgar just stared in shock for another moment before recoiling. He pulled out of her and buckled his pants as he stumbled backwards.

"You're a red witch." His eyes were so wide, the whites clear even in the darkness. Remy heard his thundering heart and smelled his white-hot fear.

"Edgar." Remy didn't know what to say. That he shouldn't fear her?

"Stay away from me." His hands were shaking.

"Edgar, please," Remy said. Her chest felt cracked open by the look on his face, not only horror, but also disgust. He had slept with a witch, and now he seemed sickened with himself.

Edgar was already making his way to the door, abandoning his candle in haste. Remy wanted to chase after him, but she knew that would only make him run faster. How could he be terrified of her? The cobbler's son knew her better than almost anyone. He should have known she never wanted to hurt him.

Gut clenching, she wanted to shout to him that this was a secret, that he shouldn't tell anyone. But that look in his eyes told her she had lost him. She needed to get back to their lodgings right away. Gods, she would have to tell Heather what happened. Fenrin was going to kill her, and Heather would be so disappointed. Remy considered just fleeing into the woods and never returning rather than face that disheartened look on her guardian's face.

But she couldn't leave them in this town now that Edgar knew she was a red witch. The respectable brown witches would be tarnished by association with her. It might even be dangerous for them.

Remy cleaned herself up with the underwear in her pocket and threw it to the ground, discarded. She couldn't bring it back with her. Heather couldn't know she was having sex on top of everything else. Remy had to ask the courtesans about the herbs they used to prevent pregnancy. She had to forage for them alone because the brown witches would surely know what she was using them for. Right now, that was the least of her concerns. They needed to get out of this town, now.

CHAPTER SIX

R emy had kept too many secrets. Everything was falling apart and all because she had just wanted a little freedom.

She ran straight through the pitch-black forest. She heard Edgar at the other edge of the woods, still struggling to find his way out. At least that would buy them some time.

Her footsteps faltered as she rushed down the road. She looked up to the dark night sky. Her eyes scanned the splintering doorways and peeling paint of the houses of their street, searching for answers. What was she going to say when she got back to the apartment?

She heaved another breath, debating if she should disappear into the night. She knew how to survive in hiding now. She would be able to get by without Heather and Fenrin.

Remy shook her head, breaking into a run again. She couldn't do it. Not like this. Heather and Fenrin would be terrified that Remy was in danger. They would go looking for her.

Remy made no effort to be quiet as she slammed open

the windowpane of their apartment. Fenrin sat up from the couch, blinking away sleep.

"What's going on?" he asked, rubbing the palm of his hand into his eye socket.

"I'm sorry, Fen," Remy said, swallowing the lump in her throat.

"What did you do?" Fenrin was instantly on his feet, making his way to his hiking pack against the wall.

Even after nearly three years in this town, they packed their bags every night. They were always ready to pick up and move again. Remy had thought Heather was ridiculous for making them do it. It made sense when she was young and didn't have as much control over her magical glow, but she was an adult now. Surely, she could exist without detection. . . .

Curse the Gods. Remy hated herself.

She had done this to them. She was the reason they were fleeing in the night. Again. This time it wasn't because she was a child with no self-control. No, she was an adult. She made a choice, a foolish choice. She knew sneaking off with Edgar was dangerous. She had been so cocky that she could handle it. And now she had brought this panic into their house once more.

Fenrin didn't wait for Remy's reply before hustling to Heather's bedroom door and opening it.

"Heather, we gotta go," he said loudly, waking their guardian.

Heather was up and on her feet within an instant. She came into the room in her nightgown, arms folded. Her copper-red hair was plaited in a sleeping braid, draped over her shoulder.

"What happened?" she asked. Her face shaped into a frown, but her eyes looked at Remy with worry. Remy knew

41

Heather's eyes could see it all. Her guardian could see the restraint Remy was using not to glow even then.

"Edgar found out about me," Remy said, looking down to her hands. She wouldn't tell them how he found out about her, but she was sure they would be able to guess. Red witch magic glowed for all sorts of heightened emotions, but she knew they would guess which one.

"Edgar? The cobbler's boy?" Heather hissed. Remy picked at her fingers.

"*That's* where you were going?" Fenrin growled. Remy picked at the skin around her thumbnail hard enough that it started to bleed. She didn't want to cry in front of them.

She didn't think Fenrin would ever forgive her this time. He had warned her not to be reckless, and she had done it anyway. She kept destroying these witches' lives over and over again. She didn't deserve them.

"You knew she was sneaking out?" Heather whirled on Fenrin.

"Why are you getting mad at me?" Fenrin balked.

Heather took a long breath, trying and failing to clear her frustration, eyes darting to Remy.

"Can I speak with you for a moment?" Her guardian's tone made Remy swallow the lump in her throat. Heather cut Fenrin a look. "Keep packing."

Each step into the bedroom made Remy feel an inch smaller as Heather shut the door behind them. Heather moved past her, sitting on the bed they had shared for nearly the past three years. Remy stood staring at her guardian for a long time. She wondered how long the silence would stretch on between them. Every second it became more unbearable until Remy had to speak.

"I don't think he'll say anything, Heather," Remy

blurted out. "He is probably too scared. We could go talk to him and—"

"We are leaving," Heather insisted.

"We can leave in the morning," Remy said. "Really, I don't think that it will be that bad."

Her words felt hollow even to her own ears.

"It was almost time to go anyway." Heather looked down to her hands.

"I. . . ." Remy swallowed again. She didn't know what to say to her. "I didn't mean for this to happen."

She braced for Heather's hard look, but when her guardian looked up her hazel eyes were filled with tears. Remy's chest seized at that. It was so much worse than bearing her anger. She had done this to Heather.

"You're eighteen Remy, I don't know what I could have expected," Heather said. Remy looked away. "I take it, we both know *how* Edgar discovered your magic?"

Gods, she wished the floor would open under her and swallow her whole. She nodded to Heather.

"And you're taking precautions?" Heather's voice was so soft it made Remy's hands shake. She could feel the weight of her guardian's disappointment like it thickened the air.

"I am," Remy said.

Heather bobbed her chin and released a long breath. "I wish you had told me."

Remy shook her head as Heather stood up and walked over to her. "I didn't know how to tell you. I knew you would try to stop me."

Heather's shoulders drooped. She would have tried. There was no denying that.

"I know the way we live makes you feel like you're not even allowed to exist in the world. I hope one day that won't be true," Heather said, reaching up and cupping Remy's cheek. "But you are too important to this world Remy. I'm sorry that this sheltered life is so stifling but," she took a ragged breath, "you need to survive."

There it was again. The weight of who she was.

"I don't want to hide anymore," she whispered, stepping out of Heather's grasp.

"I know," Heather murmured. "But you have us. You are not alone, Remini."

Remy's eyes snapped up to Heather's. "Don't call me that."

She was about to say something more when she pulled up short. Her eyes darted out to the window. The sound of angry voices echoed from outside. They had come to kill her.

Humans might fear her power, but they loved money more. King Vostemur would pay them bags of gold for her head. It was enough money to feed the whole town for years.

"Do you see what you've done?" Fenrin snarled as they rushed back into the living room.

Remy peeked out the side window, looking toward the front steps. Four men stood crowded around the building's entrance. Their apartment was the first door on the right. Witches knew it was an unlucky door, but it had been the only one available so they took it.

Three more men joined the crowded circle on the stoop. They crossed their arms and spoke quietly to each other, planning something.

Remy's eyes snagged on a mop of blond hair at the back. Edgar.

The stout man to his right was the town cobbler, his father. Remy had seen the others in the tavern before but didn't know their names.

"Shit," she cursed, pulling back the curtains as more men emerged from the darkness. "There's ten of them now."

"We'll go out the back window," Heather said. She took two *druni* from her pack and smacked them down on the table. Only a select few humans would recognize the gesture. They called it "a witch's goodbye". They would see the two silver coins and know the witches were gone. They had left many witch's goodbyes over their years in hiding.

Heather began frantically pulling the drying herbs from the ceiling. Fenrin shoved the last of the brown vials into his pack. Remy wished she had worn underwear, but there was no time for that now. She tied up her three caught rabbits to her pack. It was all she needed to do and she was ready to go.

They heard more loud voices and Remy peeked out again, gripping her bow tighter in her hand.

"There's more now." She frowned. That was a lot of angry humans.

A loud pounding sounded on the door to their apartment. One of the other tenants must have let them in the building's locked front entrance. They would find no allies here.

"Give us the red witch and we will spare you brown witches!" came a booming shout.

Fenrin snorted as he put on his pack and lifted the second one into his hands. They all knew it was a lie. If they stayed, they would all be dead.

They began to move to the back room just as Remy heard the man at the door say, "go around the back."

"They're out the back too," Remy warned in a hushed tone.

Fenrin whirled around. His eyes shot to the window in the kitchen, then back through the doorway to the bedroom, scanning the exits.

"We'll have to fight our way out then," he said, wide-eyed. Fenrin was not a fighter. He was big, sure, and he could break up a bar fight. But he never took a swing at anyone, even when they deserved it. Heather wasn't a fighter either. She was tough as nails when she needed to be, but she would be no help against twenty angry humans. So that left Remy.

Remy felt the arrows jostling in her quiver. There were only six left. She had been planning on making more soon. Six arrows against twenty men were terrible odds. Of course, she also had her magic, though she was never allowed to use it. What could she possibly do with the power to move and animate objects? It took an incredible amount of mental strength just to move one object at a time. Once her power was depleted, she wouldn't be able to use it again until she had rested. Remy couldn't hold them all off. Even if she could, Heather would never forgive her. Heather had always worried what Remy could do if she ever unleashed her powers. Remy was never afforded the chance to find out.

Sweeping her copper braid behind her back, Heather lifted her chin. She stomped her foot down hard and the floorboard beneath her boot sprang up, it's rusty nail giving way.

Fenrin and Remy just gaped at their guardian as she said, "Let's go."

For all her motherly ways, Heather was still a witch, clever and cunning as anything. Fenrin hustled over to her and pried up two more boards with ease. He took off his pack and dropped into the hole. It wasn't much of a drop for such a tall person. From the waist up, he was still in the room. Good. At least there would be enough space for them to crawl out from under the house.

They passed their heavy packs down to Fenrin, one for each of them plus the pack of their brown witch goods. Then Fenrin helped Heather into the hole. The pounding on the door was getting louder. People were beginning to shout as Remy dropped into the open floor. She kept her bow tucked tightly to her back as she surveyed the under-side of their townhouse.

The whole bottom of the building was covered in old wrap-around trellising. Climbing weeds and cobwebs clung to each frame. She could see the shuffling feet of boots through the trellis. They wrapped around the front right corner of the building where the witches' apartment was located. No one had thought to go to the far side where the other tenants lived.

Heather was already making her way across the dirty ground, dragging two packs with her. Fenrin pulled two of the floorboards back in place and then grabbed the thread-bare rug from under the kitchen sink. He pulled the last floorboard through the hole and turned to Remy.

"Put the rug over the boards," he whispered.

Remy's mouth dropped open.

"I can't!" she hissed.

"Yes, you can," Fenrin insisted, looking over Remy's shoulder to see that Heather was far enough away. "Cover the boards."

Remy clenched her shaking hands into fists. They were already faintly glowing as the adrenaline tore through her body. She pushed out her thread of red magic, feeling a line of warm buzzing spool out of her and up to the floor above. She held the rug in her mind's eye. Willing it to move, she heard the faint brushing sound as it shifted into place.

"Good," Fenrin gritted out, grabbing his pack and moving.

Remy wondered if it would ever be the same between them. She didn't think he would let it go so easily this time.

She grabbed her pack, dragging it through the loose dirt. She crouched to keep her head from hitting the floor above her. Fenrin had to waddle in a squat, contorting his gangly body to fit in the tight space.

Remy flinched for a second as she heard the door above them burst open. They had beaten it down.

"Give us the red witch!" a voice shouted.

"Give us her head!" another few shouted as they stampeded into the room above.

They had reached the far end of the house. The bloodthirsty shouts had quieted as they looked for the witches only to find an empty apartment. Maybe they would just chalk it up to magic. Maybe they would believe that the witches could evaporate into the ether. But it wasn't worth staying to find out.

Heather pushed down the far trellising with barely a nudge, the weeds the only things keeping it in place. The brown witch took a deep breath and cast her eyes to Remy and then Fenrin.

"We run to the woods. We take the trail south until we get to the main road. Then we'll make a plan," Heather instructed them. "Ready?"

This was what Heather did best. In the panic all around them, she was calm and steady. A mob of angry humans was champing at the bit to kill them, and here was Heather, a mighty redwood in a windstorm. She looked at

Remy and Fenrin the same way she did when they were young, like it was all going to be okay. Remy needed to hear that from her guardian even now. That need probably never went away.

Heather ran out, quick for her small size and the weight of the pack on her shoulders. Remy and Fenrin dashed out behind her. The woods were only a short sprint away.

"There!" a voice shouted. Remy could feel the weight of a dozen eyes upon them. The witches refused to slow down.

They breached into the tree line with incredible speed as the mob began to thunder after them. Heather moved with an easy grace, even in the darkness, but Fenrin's foot snagged on a root, and he went down. Remy scrambled to him, hoisting him back up.

"Red Witch!" Remy knew the voice that screamed right behind her.

Fenrin's eyes darted over Remy's shoulder, his pupils dilating in fear.

"Run, Fen," Remy growled, shoving him onward.

Fenrin turned, bolting on spindly legs. Remy did not follow.

She spun, snatching an arrow out of her quiver and nocking it as she turned. The arrowhead pointed straight at Edgar. Another two men ran up behind him. The rest were hustling out of the townhouse and would reach them in seconds.

"So brave now, aren't you Edgar?" Remy asked, feeling the buzz of magic behind her eyes. She knew the three men before her hesitated, not because of her bow and arrow but because of the glow.

Edgar had nearly pissed himself when he discovered what she was. Now, with twenty men behind him, he acted like he was some kind of hero. Remy refused to let him see the sting from the hateful way he said *red witch*. She wouldn't give him the satisfaction.

Blinking back her tears of frustration, Remy gritted her teeth. She never thought Edgar would do this to her. Just hours ago, he had looked at her like she was the moon in the sky and now he looked at her like she was a demon. She had let him know her in such intimate ways, more than anyone else. He had been her first in every way, apart from that one peck of a kiss when she was fifteen. And here he was now, ready to kill her with his bare hands.

The mob thundering up behind the three men paused when they saw her scarlet beams of light emanating from the darkness of the woods. They looked at Remy as if she were the Goddess of Death.

She imagined it in her mind's eye, that she was the fearsome goddess. She pretended she was holding a new bow, red flames licking up her arms, her eyes shining red. She wore the leathers of a fae warrior, knee high boots and a belt of daggers, long hair shimmering in the pre-dawn air. The Goddess was formidable and venerated, the perfect image of the fighter she needed to be.

"You're going to die, Witch," Edgar snarled.

Her fingers skimmed the red thread around her fletching. She wanted to crack under the hateful look in Edgar's eyes but instead she just smirked like the monster they feared her to be and released her arrow.

CHAPTER SEVEN

The arrow whizzed through the shadows, striking
Edgar below his collarbone. She had been aiming
for his shoulder, a warning shot, but in her anger,
she hadn't been paying enough attention. The sound that
Edgar made as he gasped made Remy fear she had punctured his lung.

Blood pooled down his tunic as his eyes went wide. His
knees knocked hard into the ground.

Two men lurched forward, moving around Edgar.
Remy thought they would have stopped to help their friend,
but they went after her instead. All they saw was the biggest
payday of their lives.

Remy didn't pause as she shot them, hitting one in the
arm and one in the thigh in rapid succession. Better shots.
She didn't want to kill them, refusing to be the demon they
feared. They cried out, clutching their hands to the arrows
stabbed into their bodies. Crimson liquid streamed down
their clothing, a deluge of blood, but the two of them would
survive it.

Edgar, however. Her former lover lay on the ground,

gasping.

Gods, that arrow was so low in his chest. She had nearly pierced his heart. Edgar wanted her dead but this . . . this was not who Remy was. She didn't want to be the reason he died. She had the urge to run over to him, yank out her arrow, and staunch the bleeding. She took one step toward him, and Edgar grabbed the knife at his belt. With trembling, bloody hands he pointed it at her. He must have thought she was advancing to kill him. The panic in his pale blue eyes was clear even in the darkness. He was terrified of her.

Remy's hands started shaking as she stared at his haunted face. Maybe he had never really wanted her. Maybe he had just wanted a pretty girl to satisfy his lust. There couldn't have been real feelings. Not if he looked at her the way he did now. The pain in her chest was so acute, she felt as if an arrow stabbed through her too. She had never loved him, so why did it hurt so much?

The mob that had paused was slowly advancing. Each heartbeat they inched closer to her. All it would take was for one to make their move and then they would all be running at her.

Remy dropped her eyebrows heavy over her glowing eyes as she snarled at them. She had three arrows left.

She darted looks from one person to the next, the magic inside her raging. She yearned to lash out at each of them, to see what her magic could do. How far could she push herself if only she allowed it? How mighty could she be? Maybe she could pull down a giant tree from magic alone. The people in this shitty town, they should pay for her suffering.

"Remy!" She could hear Fenrin's desperate call from deep in the woods. He must have realized she wasn't right behind him anymore. She needed to hurry and catch up, otherwise she knew they would turn back for her. She wasn't willing to put the brown witches in front of an angry mob. Vengeance would have to wait. She wasn't the Goddess of Death; she was just a young witch. That beautiful vision in her mind, the powerful warrior she wished she could be, would have to wait for another day.

With one last glowing red look, Remy turned and sprinted back into the woods. The mob raced after her as if her running broke the spell on them. She willed her magic out behind her to the trees. Leaves rustled and wood creaked as the branches wove together behind her, blocking the trail.

Gasps and shouts echoed behind her as the men watched the enchanted trees. That should slow them down. Maybe they would turn back entirely.

If the magic trees didn't stop them, the darkness surely would. It was still another hour until sunrise, and the forest was so dark that a human wouldn't be able to see their hand in front of their face. But Heather and Fenrin lived in the night, and they were used to navigating forest trails in the pitch black . . . because of Remy. She was the reason they had become so skilled at fleeing in the dark.

Remy caught up to her companions within seconds and took the lead using her fear to light the path with her radiant red light. They fell into this same configuration so easily because they'd been doing it for years. Remy pushed down on the guilt threatening to override her body. She would grieve her actions once they were safe again. She bristled at that notion.

She would never be safe.

$\approx$

The sun had reached the horizon by the time they made it through the wood and onto the high road. No one followed them. Remy's red magic was enough to frighten them away. Her magic was thoroughly spent, though. The adrenaline had made Remy push her magic to its limits. Now she was exhausted. It would probably be weeks before she could conjure her magic again, not that Heather would ever allow it.

Remy braced herself for Heather's lecture. She knew as soon as they were safe again it would be coming.

They trudged along the main road, dust kicking up in their wake. The utter silence of Heather and Fenrin pressed in on Remy with an unkind weight. She didn't know where to begin. Apologizing didn't feel like nearly enough, but she didn't want to give them an explanation either. Remy thought back to Edgar, of that arrow landing so close to his heart.

She prayed to the Moon Goddess that she had not punctured his lung and that he would be swiftly healed. Of course, the two brown witches with the magical healing elixirs had just been driven out of town with her so it would not heal as quickly as it could have. Even if he had looked like he wanted to kill Remy, it didn't excuse her killing him. He had looked at her like she was a demon and she had played the part so well. She could imagine how terrifying she looked to them: hands and eyes glowing red, shooting arrows with incredible aim. She was a nightmare made flesh.

Remy promised herself that she would be more inconspicuous in the next town. She wouldn't talk to anyone. She wouldn't meet the eye of a single person. She had learned her lesson again and again. This is what people saw when they looked too closely at her: a glowing red demon.

A wagon turned the corner on the road behind them. The three of them spun in unison to see a large open wagon being pulled by two old horses. The wheels squeaked, and the wagon wobbled like a ship on stormy seas, but it was fast moving.

Heather raised a hand, waving to the driver. He was an older man, greying at the temples, with a large salt and pepper beard. He wore a wide-brimmed hat to protect from the sun and a dirty shirt with rolled-up sleeves. Pulling the horses to a halt, he surveyed Heather, and then his eyes lingered on Remy. Averting her gaze, Remy looked anywhere but at the human man. No more looking at humans. They could sense that something was not quite right about her.

"Please, sir," Heather said, the witch accent disappearing from her voice as she put on the act of a fawning human, "Would we please be able to hitch a ride?"

"Where are you headed?" the man asked, shifting uncomfortably in his seat.

"Where are you going?" Heather countered. The man reached up to scratch the back of his head. His other hand moving to scratch his leg.

"I'm on a long haul, heading southeast to deliver some grain. Probably about three more hours," he said, unable to sit still.

"Excellent, that is where we are heading as well." Heather smiled warmly.

"It's a lot of extra weight to haul the three of you as far as Harbruck," the man hedged. Remy knew this was the part where they needed to sweeten the deal.

Heather eyed up the man and without missing a beat said, "How about a cure for that rash you have?"

The man blanched, looking at Heather more suspi-

ciously now. It wouldn't take a witch to know that he was
covered in some sort of rash, the way he jostled and itched.
Heather rummaged around in the pack Fenrin had rested
against his knees, pulling out a small, brown vial and
holding it up to the man.

"If you drink this, the itching will have ended before we
board your wagon and the rash will be gone by the time you
reach your destination," she promised. This was the ease of
the witch. Their goods and services sold themselves.
Everyone was willing to trust them just enough to take their
misery away. When you were scratching yourself raw, you'd
do anything for a cure.

The man looked at Remy again, his eyes drifting to the
back of her pack.

"Throw in those rabbits and you've got yourself a deal,"
he said.

"Done," Remy replied, untying the three rabbits and
dropping them by his feet.

Heather passed over the brown bottle and the man took
it almost too eagerly. He uncorked it, swigging it down.
Fenrin moved to the back of the wagon and tossed up his
two packs, then grabbed Heather's and tossed it back onto
the bags of grain. Remy thought he wouldn't offer to take
her pack, not after everything that had just happened
between them. But sure enough, her friend grabbed her bag
off her shoulders and tossed it onto the wagon. The action
was enough to make Remy's chest tighten. She had failed
him again.

"You're a bloody good witch, you," the man said with a
sigh, sagging with relief. True to her word, the itching had
stopped. His face blanketed with an easy smile. Little did
he know that the potion also made people calm and compla-
cent. It was worth adding a little sleeping thistle to every

elixir, just in case. Working with contented and pliable humans made every witch's life easier. It was definitely an asset in the taverns to counteract those who became violent with drink. But Remy was certain the wagon driver would have taken the elixir, regardless.

"You two ride in the back," Heather said, her brows furrowing slightly as she added, "Try to get some rest. We might be traveling a long while still."

Remy's shoulders sagged. It was all Heather needed to say to let her know of her disappointment. She had dragged them out of their beds at night and made them flee for their lives again. Remy turned without a word and hopped up onto the back of the rickety wagon. She sat between two massive bags of grain that dwarfed her in size. Good. People wouldn't be able to spy her on the road. Though she doubted anyone from that seedy town would bother hunting her down further than the village limits. They were all barely surviving as it was. They didn't have time to go chasing witches through the Western Court—that was a job for the fae.

Fenrin climbed up onto the back of the wagon, sitting himself across from Remy. His height was so tall that his head peeked up over the giant grain stores. He pushed his feet into a pack across from him, bracing himself to be jostled.

The wagon jolted to life. Remy lurched forward. She pushed her feet down hard onto the wagon floor to keep from sliding. This would be a long three hours. Heather and the wagon driver broke out into a facile, uncomplicated conversation. They chatted about the weather and how it's been a good summer and of the abundance of fruit crops this year.

Remy thought to the blackberry bushes Fenrin had

planted by their secret lookout. The brambles would probably take over that fallen log untended, blocking the spectacular view. Remy would never see it again. She hadn't been prepared to say goodbye to those waterfalls and the spirits of her ancestors that resided on the other side of that mountain. Now they were driving even further from her homeland toward the southeast. Every mile was another string cut from who she really was. She doubted she and Fenrin would have another secret special place. She didn't know if they'd even be friends anymore.

That thought crushed her even more than driving away from her homeland. The spirits of her ancestors were all abstract beings to her. Fenrin was her real flesh and blood friend. His dismissal would hurt her more than the shame of the fallen family she never got to know.

Her face burned with shame, tears pricking her eyes as a hard rock built in her throat. Her nostrils flared as she bit down hard on the inside of her cheek to keep the tears from welling. But she was unsuccessful. Thick hot droplets fell down her face as she hung her head, hiding even from herself.

She felt Fenrin shift. He stood into a crouch, nearly toppling over like a baby deer as the wagon rocked. He moved across to her and wedged himself between Remy and a bag of grain. They wedged together so tightly, arms and hips pressed conjointly, that they stopped sliding around. It was a relief that they wouldn't have to brace themselves the whole ride, but the move made Remy's tears flow faster. As she heaved silent sobs, Fenrin wrapped his long arm around her and pulled her into his lean chest. Remy rested her face on him, soaking his tunic in her tears. He stroked slow circles around her back.

"I will plant us some more blackberry bushes at the next

place," he said, somehow knowing exactly what was breaking her spirit. Remy nodded into his chest as she swallowed that thick knot in her throat.

She clung to him tighter, her friend. He should not have been so kind. She did not deserve his kindness, but she accepted it gratefully.

"What about a library?" Fenrin said as the last of Remy's tears fell and she began to feel more in her body again.

She pulled back to look at Fenrin. "A library?" she repeated with a confused frown.

"Our palace has to have a library. We haven't discussed what it would look like yet," he said with a smirk. It was more of a peace offering than anything else he could say. That sweet offer made Remy want to cry again.

"Yes, of course," she said with a half-smile. Wiping the residual wetness from under her eyes, she pulled her head away from his chest so she could see him. "I'm thinking it has to be at least two stories."

"At the very least." Fenrin nodded with a feigned expression of seriousness.

"And there will be ladders on wheels that we can use to find the perfect book," Remy insisted.

"And two giant armchairs by an enormous window with sweeping views over our estate," Fenrin added.

"Yes." Remy smiled, imagining the daydream in her head. "And a huge fireplace for reading by in the winters. So we can read long into the night."

"Very good point," Fenrin mused.

They carried on with their daydream, planning every detail of their library down to where each genre would be located and how they would organize their books. They talked about the type of wood they would use to build the shelves and colors of the rugs that would dot the main floor. They talked about how the second-floor balcony would have a golden painted railing and that there would be a secret reading nook behind the adventure books.

They talked for hours, the time seeming to fade away along with the nightmare of the evening before. Remy would let the worries haunt her another day, but today she would plan her glorious library. They planned all the way to the town the wagon-driver spoke of, Harbruck.

It was a medium-sized town, not too far off the main road, but far enough that there wouldn't be many fae travelers stopping through. It had more shops, freshly painted signs hung above the doorways. The road was clean, no weeds sprung up from the cracks in the ground. It was a country town like all the others, but at least it didn't reek of urine. Maybe there would be better accommodation too. Maybe the tavern staff would be nicer. Remy knew it didn't matter. They would stay here until it was time to move on again.

Heather had told Remy she was too important to keep being reckless. Remy wondered when it would be time to start being important. Or would she have to hide away in these little towns for the rest of her life?

The wagon driver had been so enchanted by his conversations with Heather that he had given her a bag of oats and dropped them off directly in front of the town tavern. Remy looked up at the building. It was dusty and somewhat neglected, but it was still in far better condition than some of the taverns they had stayed in. A wooden sign hung above the door, paint peeling off the red oxide lettering: Rusty Hatchet.

"How charming," Fenrin said, giving Remy a wink.

Remy rolled her eyes, stretching her cramped legs as she stood. Her body was tired and her soul even more so. She looked back up at the Rusty Hatchet as she stretched her neck. She wondered how many years they would last this time before she was discovered again. She was always discovered again.

Thank you so much for reading Remy's story! Find out what happens next in *The High Mountain Court: The Five Crowns of Okrith Book 1*

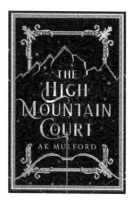

If you enjoyed reading this story, please consider sharing on social media or telling a friend! Happy reading!

ABOUT THE AUTHOR

AK Mulford lives in the perfect place for a fantasy author: New Zealand! Mulford grew up craving seeing herself represented in the world of fantasy and is inspired to create diverse and LGBTQ+ fantasy stories that transport readers to new realms of imagination, helping them to fall in love with fantasy for the first time, or, all over again. A former primatologist,  Mulford has now swapped raising monkeys for writing fantasy. She lives in Wellington with her husband and two wonderful young kids. In her down time (what is this mythical "down time"?), she spends time with her cat and dog, and makes ridiculous and fun Tiktok videos.

www.akmulford.com

ACKNOWLEDGMENTS

Thank you to my family for always encouraging me. Without your support these stories would have never made it onto the page. I love you all.

To the amazing community of friends I have made on Tiktok: thank you for all of your support and welcoming me into the best bookish community around! I am grateful for each and every one of you. Right, okay, back to lip-syncing and goofing off. #Ily

To Hayley, thank you for beta reading for me and being the self-appointed president of my fan club. I am so grateful to have you in my life. Love you babe.

To my crispy taco delights, thanks for always being in my corner and getting me through the tough days! I don't know what I would do without you.

Thank you to Hannah Close from Reedsy for her editing services and for elevating my story with her editorial assessment.

I would like to thank Meadow Lamoreaux from Rose City Editing for her editing services

Thank you to Norma Gambini from Normas Nook

Proofreading for all of your support and amazing proof-reading skills.

Thank you to Kristen Timofeev for the beautiful map!

Thank you to MiblArt for the amazing cover.

And lastly, I'd like to thank Ziggy, my gorgeous labradoodle, for being the most patient, loving dog in the world and for not getting mad at me those times when I was too deep in a story and made him wait for breakfast.

ALSO BY AK MULFORD

The High Mountain Court

The Witches' Blade

Printed in Great Britain
by Amazon

85239220R00043